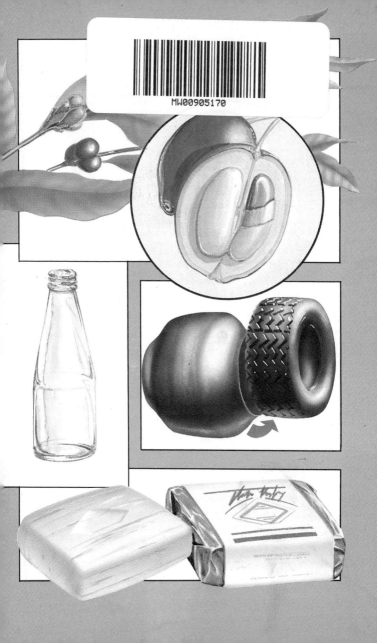

Have you ever wondered how a book is printed, or how glass is made? This exciting and informative book uses simple diagrams and colour photographs to explain how materials such as oil, sand and plants are turned into everyday objects.

Acknowledgments:
The publishers would like to thank the following organisations for their help in the preparation of this book: Allied Bakeries Ltd, A Barker and Sons Ltd, Berol Ltd, British Steel PLC, British Wool Marketing Board, Cadbury Ltd, Dartington Crystal, Dunlop International Technology Ltd, European Aspirin Foundation, International Coffee Organization, International Institute for Cotton, Lever Brothers Ltd, Levi Strauss Ltd (UK), London Brick Company Ltd, Malaysian Rubber Producers' Research Association, Mono Containers Ltd, The Nestlé Company Ltd, Oneida Silversmiths, Proctor and Gamble Educational Services, Pura Foods Ltd, Rexel Ltd, Richardson Sheffield Ltd, Royal Doulton Ltd, The Tea Council Ltd, Towles Hosiery Ltd, Staedtler, United Glass Ltd, Van den Berghs and Jurgens, The Wiggins Teape Group Ltd.

The publishers would also like to thank Wendy Body for acting as reading level consultant.

Photographic credits:
Pages 38-39, Allied Bakeries Ltd; pages 24-25, British Wool Marketing Board; page 42, External Services Department, Cadbury Ltd; pages 8-9, 14-15, 22-23, 29, 36, Tim Clark; page 26, International Institute for Cotton; pages 30-31, London Brick Company Ltd; page 18, Malaysian Rubber Producers' Research Association; page 20, Mono Containers Ltd; pages 12-13, Royal Doulton Ltd; pages 34-35, Science Photo Library; page 40, The Tea Council Ltd; page 16, United Glass Ltd.
Designed by Gavin Young.

British Library Cataloguing in Publication Data

Ganeri, Anita
    How it's made.
    1. Manufacture
    I. Title   II. Quigley, Sebastian   III. Dillow, John
    670
    ISBN 0-7214-1227-0

First edition

Published by Ladybird Books Ltd Loughborough Leicestershire UK
Ladybird Books Inc Auburn Maine 04210 USA

Printed in England (3)

How It's Made

written by ANITA GANERI

illustrated by
SEBASTIAN QUIGLEY and JOHN DILLOW

Ladybird Books

How it's made

If you look around your home or school you will see that the things you use, or eat or drink every day, are made from many different materials.

Natural products are made from plants or animals.

Paper and pencils come from wood.

Bread is made from different types of grain.

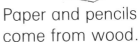

Jumpers can be made from sheep's wool.

Coffee, chocolate and tea all come from plants.

Other things are made from chemicals. These are **synthetic** or man-made products.

Plastic yogurt pots and nylon clothes are made from chemicals found in oil.

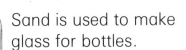

Sand is used to make glass for bottles.

Some medicines come from chemicals, others come from plants.

This book shows you how some of these everyday objects are produced.

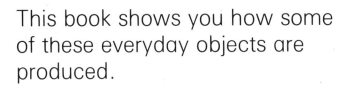

How paper is made

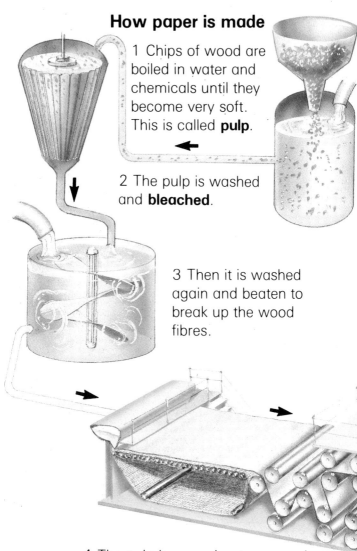

1 Chips of wood are boiled in water and chemicals until they become very soft. This is called **pulp**.

2 The pulp is washed and **bleached**.

3 Then it is washed again and beaten to break up the wood fibres.

4 The pulp is spread out over a wire mesh and shaken to remove some of the water.

Paper

The first paper was invented in Egypt about 5,000 years ago. It was made of flattened reeds and called papyrus. Today, paper is usually made from spruce, pine and eucalyptus trees.

5 A machine squeezes out the rest of the water, dries the paper and winds it onto huge rolls.

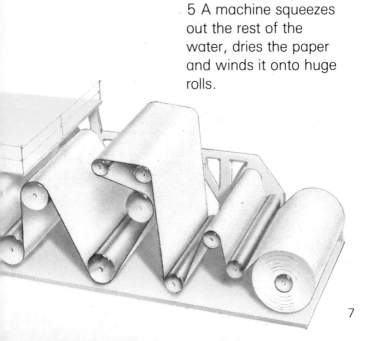

Books and comics

Books and comics are printed by machines called presses on large sheets or rolls of paper. Modern printing presses can print thousands of books, comics or newspapers an hour.

3 The paper is cut to the right size and the pages sewn, stapled or glued together.

4 To print in colour, a printer uses black, blue, red and yellow inks. These four colours make many other colours.

Printing a book

1 The words and pictures are photographed onto metal plates and covered in ink.

2 The plates are pressed onto a 'blanket' which transfers the words and pictures onto the paper.

Pencils

Pencils are made of sticks of 'lead' sandwiched between two strips of wood. The 'lead' is not really lead. It is a mixture of **graphite** and clay, which is baked in a very hot oven.

A machine cuts grooves in flat strips of wood.

A second strip of grooved wood is glued on top.

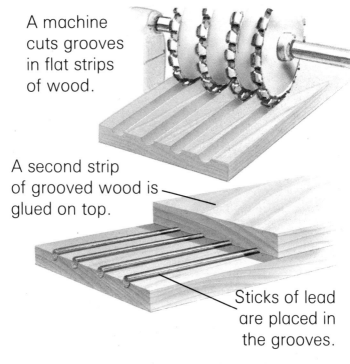

Sticks of lead are placed in the grooves.

A machine cuts one side
of the pencils into
shape.

Then the strips are
turned over and the other side is cut.

The pencils are dipped in
lacquer and then stamped
with the name of
the
company that made them.

stamp

Types of pencils

More graphite in the lead makes a pencil
softer. More clay makes it harder. The
code printed on the pencil's side will tell
you how hard the pencil is.

6H
extra hard

2H
hard

H
hard

HB
hard and
black

B
black

2B
soft and
black

How china cups are made

China is made from china clay, china stone and ox bone, mixed with water. The clay mixture is put into a machine called a pug mill. The pug mill squeezes out air bubbles.

1 To make china cups, lumps of clay are placed in moulds and pressed into shape by a machine.

2 The handles are made by pouring liquid clay into moulds. Then they are stuck onto the cups.

3 The cups are baked in a very hot oven, called a kiln.

Cups, saucers and plates

Most cups, saucers and plates are made of baked clay and are called pottery. China is the finest and most expensive type of pottery.

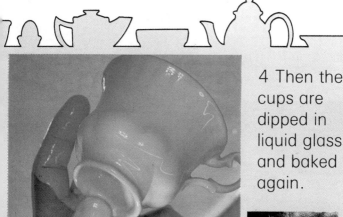

4 Then the cups are dipped in liquid glass and baked again.

5 Finally, they are decorated.

Knives

Knives are usually made from stainless steel. This is a mixture, or **alloy**, of steel and chromium. Stainless steel doesn't rust.

How a knife is made

1 A machine cuts out the blade from a long strip of steel.

2 The edge is sharpened.

3 The blade is polished...

4 ...and then dipped into chemicals to remove any dirt.

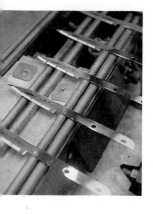

5 The name of the company and the type of knife is printed on the blade.

6 The knives are carefully tested to make sure that the blades are sharp.

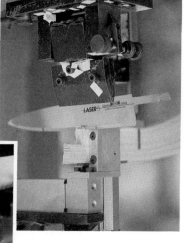

7 Finally, the plastic handle is added.

Glass bottles

It's hard to believe, but the main ingredient in glass bottles is sand! The sand is heated in a

furnace with soda and limestone until it becomes red-hot **molten** glass.

Recycled glass

Glass bottles and jars are taken from the bottle bank to a recycling centre.

Different coloured glass is sorted out and then crushed into small pieces.

Overhead magnets remove metal. Paper and plastic are removed by hand.

The crushed glass can now be made into new bottles.

How glass bottles are made

1 A gob of molten glass is dropped into a metal mould.

mould

2 Air is blown into the glass. The bottle is then taken out of the mould.

air

3 It is then placed in another mould.

mould

4 Air is blown in once more and the glass is forced into the mould to form the final bottle shape.

air

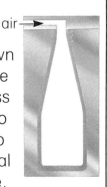

5 The bottles are slowly cooled so that they harden but don't crack.

Rubber tyres

Rubber is a very useful material. It is waterproof, flexible and can return to its original shape after stretching.

Natural rubber comes from rubber trees. Slits are cut in the tree bark and a juice called latex oozes out. Acid is added to the latex and lumps of solid rubber are formed.

collecting the latex

These items are made from natural rubber.

Today most rubber is made from chemicals. It is called synthetic rubber.

How car tyres are made

Layers of fabric covered with synthetic rubber are placed on a drum.

The fabric contains steel cords to make it strong.

A thick layer of rubber is added on top. This will form the tread and sidewalls.

The tyre is placed in a mould where it is heated and squeezed to give the correct shape.

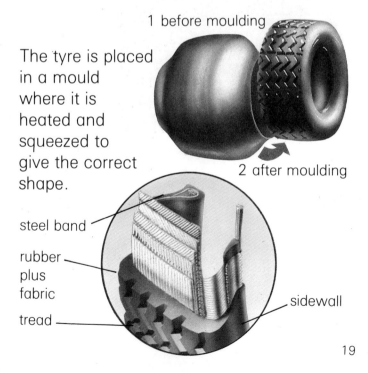

1 before moulding

2 after moulding

steel band

rubber plus fabric

tread

sidewall

19

Plastic yogurt pots

Plastic is a synthetic material made from the chemicals found in oil. These chemicals are mixed together to form small hard granules. When heated the soft

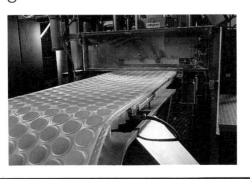

plastic can be moulded into different shapes.

How yogurt pots are made

After heating, the sheet of hot plastic is pushed into pot-shaped moulds.

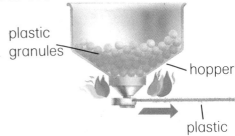

plastic granules

hopper

plastic sheet

These things are made from different kinds of plastic.

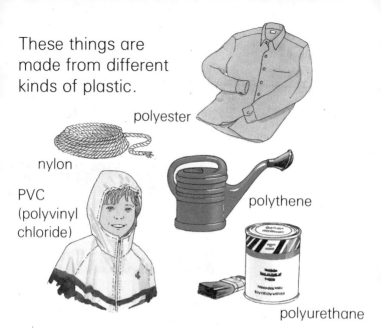

polyester

nylon

PVC (polyvinyl chloride)

polythene

polyurethane

Can you think of any more?

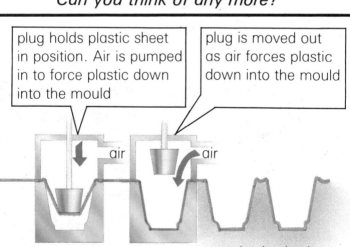

plug holds plastic sheet in position. Air is pumped in to force plastic down into the mould

plug is moved out as air forces plastic down into the mould

air

air

water cools plastic shape

Shoes

Leather is often used to make shoes because it is comfortable and helps to keep your feet cool and dry.

Shoe leather is made from the skin of animals such as cows. The skin is soaked in chemicals to remove the hairs and to stop it rotting.

The uppers are cut out and sewn together.

Then they are pulled over a **last**, and the insole is attached.

The sole is glued on. The heel is nailed to the sole.

The shoes are sprayed and polished, then packed into boxes.

The different parts of a training shoe

nylon side panels support the foot and allow it to breathe

leather fabric

carbon rubber sole helps the shoe to last longer

air cushions

grooves allow the foot to move easily

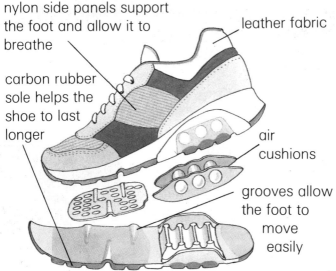

Jumpers

Your warmest jumpers are probably made of sheep's wool. Wool can also come from goats, rabbits and even camels.

1 Each year, a sheep's fleecy coat is cut off, or sheared.

2 The fleece is washed to remove grease, mud and twigs.

3 The wool is fed into a carding machine. Here it is untangled by rollers covered in tiny wire teeth. The wool comes out in long strands called slivers.

4 The slivers are twisted during spinning into long threads called yarn, and dyed.

5 Jumpers can be knitted by hand or on very fast knitting machines.

Woven cloth

Yarn is stretched in regular lines across a frame – this is called the warp. A **shuttle** is used to thread other yarn through the warp – this is called the weft.

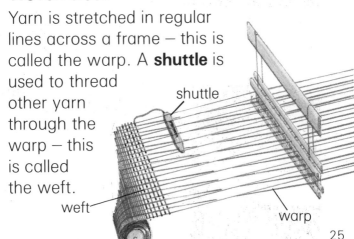

shuttle

weft

warp

Jeans

Jeans are made from a tough cotton fabric called denim.

Cotton grows inside the fruits, or bolls, of cotton plants.

When ripe, the bolls burst open. Inside, there are about thirty seeds with cotton fibres attached.

A **gin** removes the cotton fibre from the seeds.

The cotton fibres are combed to get the tangles out and spun into long threads.

The threads are dyed blue and then woven into cloth.

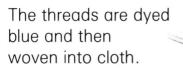

A machine cuts out the pieces of denim using a **laser** beam.

The pieces are sewn together and zips, buttons and rivets are added.

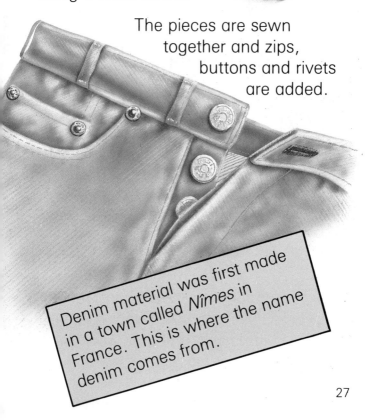

Denim material was first made in a town called *Nîmes* in France. This is where the name denim comes from.

Socks

Socks are usually knitted using nylon and wool or cotton thread. Nylon is made from plastic granules. It makes the socks tough and hardwearing.

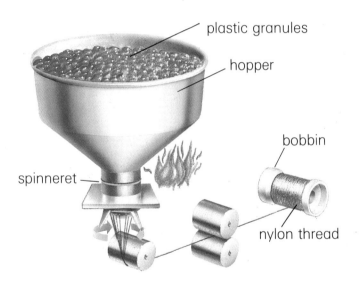

plastic granules

hopper

bobbin

spinneret

nylon thread

Plastic granules are heated and forced through holes in a **spinneret**. The thin nylon threads are twisted together and wound onto bobbins.

How socks are made

A designer or mechanic programs the sock pattern into a computer. The pattern is recorded on tape.

The tape is fed into the knitting machine and tells it how to knit the socks.

The sock comes out open at both ends.

The toe is sewn up and the sock is finished.

The fastest machines can knit a plain sock in less than two minutes.

Bricks

Today bricks are made by machine and baked in kilns.

A machine called an excavator digs clay out of the ground.

The clay is crushed into small pieces by rollers. Water, sand and coal are sometimes added.

The clay is pressed into brick shapes.